R0085582005

01/2018

W9-AXB-502

Dear Parents:

Congratulations! Your child is taking the first steps on an exciting journey. The destination? Independent reading!

STEP INTO READING® will help your child get there. The program offers five steps to reading success. Each step includes fun stories and colorful art or photographs. In addition to original fiction and books with favorite characters, there are Step into Reading Non-Fiction Readers, Phonics Readers and Boxed Sets, Sticker Readers, and Comic Readers—a complete literacy program with something to interest every child.

Learning to Read, Step by Step!

Ready to Read   Preschool–Kindergarten
• big type and easy words • rhyme and rhythm • picture clues
For children who know the alphabet and are eager to begin reading.

Reading with Help   Preschool–Grade 1
• basic vocabulary • short sentences • simple stories
For children who recognize familiar words and sound out new words with help.

Reading on Your Own   Grades 1–3
• engaging characters • easy-to-follow plots • popular topics
For children who are ready to read on their own.

Reading Paragraphs   Grades 2–3
• challenging vocabulary • short paragraphs • exciting stories
For newly independent readers who read simple sentences with confidence.

Ready for Chapters   Grades 2–4
• chapters • longer paragraphs • full-color art
For children who want to take the plunge into chapter books but still like colorful pictures.

STEP INTO READING® is designed to give every child a successful reading experience. The grade levels are only guides; children will progress through the steps at their own speed, developing confidence in their reading. The F&P Text Level on the back cover serves as another tool to help you choose the right book for your child.

Remember, a lifetime love of reading starts with a single step!

All rights reserved. Published in the United States by Random House Children's Books, a division of Penguin Random House LLC, New York. Originally published by Golden Books, an imprint of Random House Children's Books, in 1998.

Step into Reading, Random House, and the Random House colophon are registered trademarks of Penguin Random House LLC.

Visit us on the Web!
StepIntoReading.com
randomhousekids.com
RichardScarryBooks.com

Educators and librarians, for a variety of teaching tools, visit us at RHTeachersLibrarians.com

Library of Congress Cataloging-in-Publication Data
Scarry, Richard.
The worst helper ever! / by Richard Scarry. — 1st Random House ed.
  p. cm. — (Step into reading. A step 2 book)
Summary: Farmer Pig needs help on the farm, but that is not what he gets from Charlie Cat.
ISBN 978-0-307-26100-7 (trade) — ISBN 978-0-375-99990-1 (lib. bdg.)
[1. Animals—Fiction. 2. Farm life—Fiction.]
I. Title. II. Series: Step into reading. Step 2 book.
PZ7 .S327Wor 2003 [E]—dc21 2002153661

Printed in the United States of America 19 18 17 16 15 14 13 12 11 10

This book has been officially leveled by using the F&P Text Level Gradient™ Leveling System.

Richard Scarry's
The
Worst Helper
Ever!

RICHARD SCARRY'S BUSY WORLD

Random House 🏠 New York

Wake up, Farmer Pig.

It's time to go to work.

What a busy, busy day!

You need a helper,
Farmer Pig.

Hello, Charlie Cat!

Are you busy?

No, I'm not busy,
Farmer Pig.

Can you help me, Charlie Cat?

Yes, Farmer Pig.
I can drive your truck.

11

Oh, dear!
Not THAT way,
Charlie Cat.

Drive OVER the water,
not through it!

Charlie Cat,
you are the
worst helper ever!

But Farmer Fox is
a good helper.

Oh, dear!

Be careful, Charlie Cat.

No more mistakes!

Can you help me
in the barn,
Charlie Cat?

Yes, I can milk the cow,
Farmer Pig.

Oh, dear!

Not THAT way,
Charlie Cat.

Keep the milk IN the pail.
Don't spill it!

Can you help me
in the garden,
Charlie Cat?

Yes, I can water the garden,
Farmer Pig.

Oh, dear!

Not THAT way,
Charlie Cat.

Water the garden,
not the kitchen!

Please sit down,
Charlie Cat.

It's time to eat.

No more mistakes now!

Let me clear the table,
Farmer Pig.

Oh, dear!
Not THAT way,
Charlie Cat.

I am taking you back
to town, Charlie Cat.

But this time I'll drive.

We all make mistakes.

Don't we, Farmer Pig?